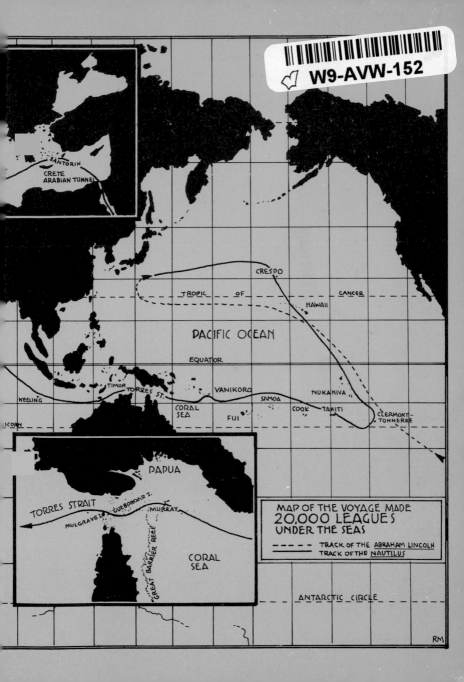

W9-AVW-152

ANTORIN
CRETE
ARABIAN TUNNEL

CRESPO

TROPIC   OF   CANCER

HAWAII

PACIFIC OCEAN

EQUATOR

TIMOR   VANIKORO   NUKAHIVA

KEELING   SAMOA   COOK   TAHITI
        TORRES ST.
        CORAL   FIJI   CLERMONT-
ICORN   SEA   TONNERRE

PAPUA

TORRES STRAIT   GUEBOROAR I.
                              MURRAY
        MULGRAVE I.
                                        CORAL
                GREAT BARRIER REEF   SEA

MAP OF THE VOYAGE MADE
20,000 LEAGUES
UNDER THE SEAS

– – – – TRACK OF THE ABRAHAM LINCOLN
———— TRACK OF THE NAUTILUS

ANTARCTIC CIRCLE

RM

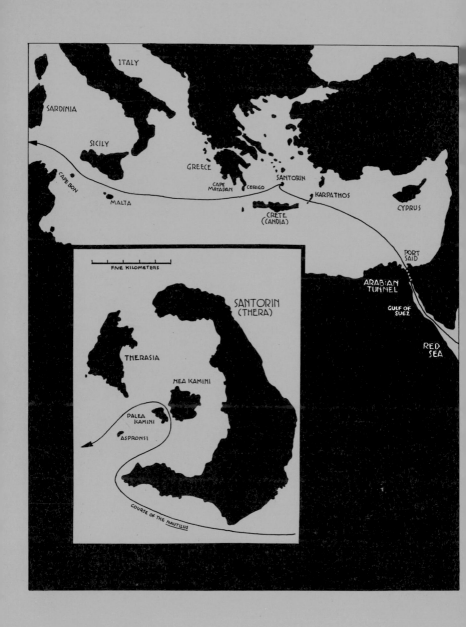

TWENTY THOUSAND LEAGUES UNDER the SEAS

TWENTY THOUSAND LEAGUES UNDER the SEAS

Illustrated by
RON MILLER
Story by Jules Verne

Translated by Ron Miller

The Unicorn Publishing House
New Jersey

Designed by Jean L. Scrocco
Edited by Heidi K. L. Corso and Ron Miller
Printed in Singapore by Singapore National Printers Ltd.
through Palace Press, San Francisco, CA
Reproduction Photography by The Color Wheel, New York, NY

♦ ♦ ♦ ♦ ♦

♦ ♦ ♦ ♦ ♦

Distributed in Canada to the book trade by Doubleday Canada, Ltd., Toronto, ON

♦ ♦ ♦ ♦ ♦

Printing History 15 14 13 12 11 10 9 8 7 6 5 4 3 2 1

♦ ♦ ♦ ♦ ♦

Library of Congress Cataloging-in-Publication Data is available.

Library of Congress Catalog Card Number: 88-32642

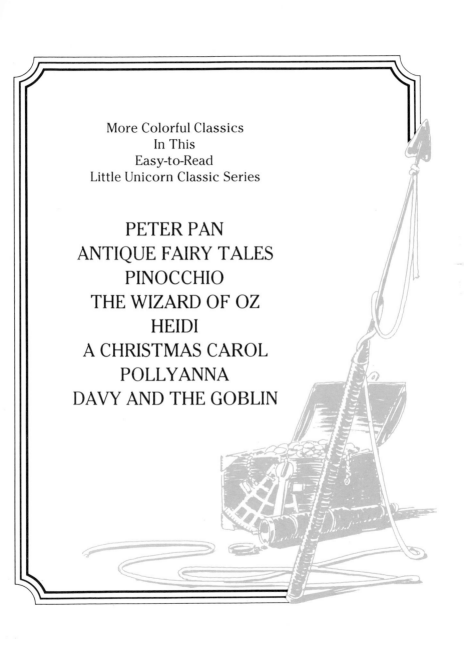

More Colorful Classics
In This
Easy-to-Read
Little Unicorn Classic Series

PETER PAN
ANTIQUE FAIRY TALES
PINOCCHIO
THE WIZARD OF OZ
HEIDI
A CHRISTMAS CAROL
POLLYANNA
DAVY AND THE GOBLIN

CAST OF CHARACTERS

David Reynolds — Captain Nemo
Tony Hardy — Conseil
Robb Kneebone — Ned Land

The Likeness of Jules Verne was used for the
character of Professor Aronnax.
Ron Miller posed for the scenes.

A sincere thank you to my friends
who posed for the unknown characters
in this edition of
Twenty Thousand Leagues Under the Seas

The Natives
The Crew of the *Nautilus*
The Crowd at the Brooklyn Pier

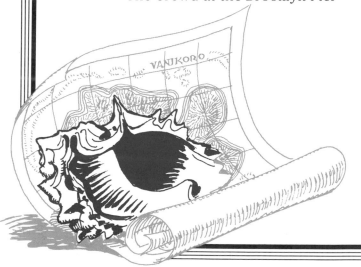

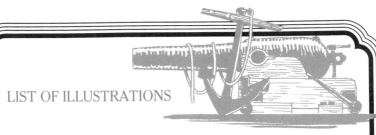

LIST OF ILLUSTRATIONS

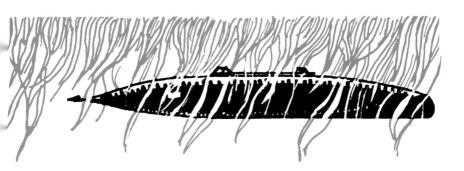

TWENTY THOUSAND LEAGUES
UNDER THE SEAS

In the year 1866, there was a big mystery. Sailors on ships all over the world had reported seeing a strange object, huge, glowing *thing*. Was it an unknown sea monster? No one knew. One ship had met the strange creature and reported that it sent two sprays of water 150 feet into the air! No whale could do that. Another time, one ship reported sighting the monster. Then, three days later another ship 2,000 miles away saw it. What sea monster could swim that fast? Finally, the captain of a steamship was able to measure the size of the monster. He thought it was more than 300 feet long! No known sea creature was that big.

What was it? The whole world wanted to know. It was in all the newspapers. Scientists argued. Could it be a whale? A giant squid? No one knew.

Soon, it became quite important to find out what the

creature was. A ship called the *Scotia* was attacked by the monster! It had been sailing along peacefully when something struck it. A big hole was punched in its side, but it was just barely able to get safely back to port. When the *Scotia* was put into dry dock to be repaired, everyone was surprised by the hole. It was a perfect triangle! What strange kind of monster could punch a hole like that through thick iron plates?

The public called for the government to do something about this dangerous creature. And that's where I came in.

My name is Professor Aronnax. I am a scientist at the Museum of Natural History in Paris, France. I was collecting samples in the American west when I first heard about the strange sea monster. The American government was sending a warship to find out what it was. Think of my surprise when I got an offer to join the journey! It seems that a scientist was needed. The Navy had liked a book I had just written about the ocean and its creatures.

Of course I accepted the offer. Taking my assistant, Conseil, with me, I went to New York where I found the ship, the *Abraham Lincoln*, waiting for me. I met the captain, Commander Farragut. He introduced me to the master harpooner who was also going on the trip. His name was Ned Land.

Soon, smoke and steam were pouring from the smokestacks. We were on our way. Hundreds of people lined the shore, waving us farewell and cheering.

Since the monster had been last seen in the Pacific Ocean, we had a long journey ahead of us. I had plenty of time to get to know Ned Land. As a scientist, I was interested in what he knew about whales. I asked him what he

thought of the monster.

"Monster! That's silly" he said.

"Don't you think there is a monster, Ned?" I asked.

"Of course not, there are no such things!"

"Well, if there is no such thing as a sea monster, what happened to the *Scotia*?"

Ned didn't have an answer to that. Soon we were in the Pacific Ocean. All eyes were glued to the sea, looking for a sign of the monster. The captain had offered a $2,000 reward for the first person to sight it. But there was no sign of it. We zigzagged back and forth for weeks, without seeing anything. The crew was starting to grumble. Finally, Commander Farragut told us that if the monster wasn't found soon, he'd give up and go home.

"This is my last chance to win that $2,000 reward!" said Ned.

"I'll just be glad to get back to Paris," said Conseil. But that night I heard Ned cry out, "There it is! The thing itself!"

Everyone rushed to the railing. There was a bright, glowing patch in the sea. The captain tried to get close to it, but it kept moving away. Soon he ordered his gunners to try and hit it. The cannons were fired, but the shells seemed to just bounce off the monster's back.

"Look out!" a sailor cried.

The monster was rushing at the ship! There was a very loud crash and I was thrown over the railing. The last thing I remember was hitting the water.

When I came to Conseil was swimming beside me. He was holding my head out of the water.

"What are you doing here?" I asked.

"I'm your assistant, wherever you go, I go too!"

Conseil was amazing! I looked around for the *Abraham Lincoln*, but it was nowhere to be seen. I thought that the monster must have sunk her, but Conseil said that the ship had just been damaged and had drifted away.

What were we to do? We were drifting in the middle of the Pacific Ocean! We swam for a long time, but it was getting harder and harder to keep afloat. Just when I thought that we were lost, I saw something dark floating in the water near us.

"Help!" I cried.

I thought I heard a voice call out. It sounded like Ned Land! As I swam closer to the dark object, I saw that it was not like any boat I had ever see. It was just a long, black hump, like half a cigar, and it was only a few feet above the water. Someone helped Conseil and me to climb onto the thing. I saw that it was Ned.

"Ned!" I said, "Were you thrown into the sea, too?"

"Yes, but I found safety right away, on this floating island."

"Island?"

"Well," Ned said, "An island made of iron!"

Sure enough, when I looked closely, I saw that the thing I was standing on was made of iron plates, pulled together. I couldn' t think of what it could be. Suddenly, the island began to move! We held onto the wet surface as best we could.

"I think it's starting to sink!" Conseil cried.

"We'll drown!" said Ned.

We started pounding on the back of the thing. Just when the waves were about to rush over us, the thing

stopped moving. There was a clanking sound, and a hatch opened. We were surprised when eight masked men came out of the machine. They carried clubs, so we didn't argue with them. They forced us through the hatch and down a ladder. We were shut up in a little iron room. We tried the door, but it was locked. We were prisoners!

Ned Land was very angry.

"Confound it!" he cried, "This is not very good treatment!"

"Calm yourself, Ned" I said, "No one has hurt us."

"Not yet!" he answered. As it was, quite some time went by before we heard the bolt on our door rattling. Two men came in. One was a short strong-looking sailor, but the other man was very tall and strong. He had a cold, intelligent look. He was the one in charge. Neither one said a word to us. I tried to speak to the tall man in every language I knew. He acted as though he didn't hear me. After a few moments, he and his companion left.

The door was locked again. "Well!" said Ned, "We spoke to those men in French, English, German and Latin! Neither one was polite enough to answer!"

"Being angry is not going to get us anywhere," I said.

"Are they going to let us starve to death?"

"We haven't been here that long," said Conseil.

We did not have long to wait. Soon the short sailor brought us a tray of food. It smelled very good.

"What do you think they eat here?" asked Ned. "Tortoise liver? Filet of shark?"

"We shall see," replied Conseil. He lifted the cover from one of the dishes. There was fish, of course, but many other things that I did not know. Everything was

very good. However, I noticed that the pieces of silverware all had the letter "N" engraved on them. What did that stand for? It was another mystery.

We slept well after our meal. However, we did not see the sailor again after we awoke, nor his mysterious commander. No one brought us food again either. Many hours went by, and Ned's anger grew greater and greater. He shouted and pounded on the iron walls and door. It did no good. I had to agree with him. If our captors were good people, this was far too long to leave us locked in.

After a whole day had gone by, we heard the lock rattling. As soon as the sailor entered, Ned threw the man to the floor and began choking him! Conseil and I were rushing to the sailor's rescue when we heard a voice.

"Please be quiet, Mister Land. And you, Professor Aronnax, will you please listen to me?"

It was the mysterious tall commander who had spoken! Ned was so surprised that he let the sailor go. The poor man left the cell. After a few moments of silence, the commander spoke again.

"Gentlemen, I speak many languages. I could have talked to you when you first spoke to me, but I wanted first to study you and to find out who you were. I was very annoyed that you have come here. I am a man who has broken all ties with the human race, and now here you are to trouble my peaceful life."

"It was an accident!" I cried.

"An accident?" he replied. "Was it an accident that your ship chased me and shot at me?"

"We didn't know what you were! We thought that you were a sea monster!"

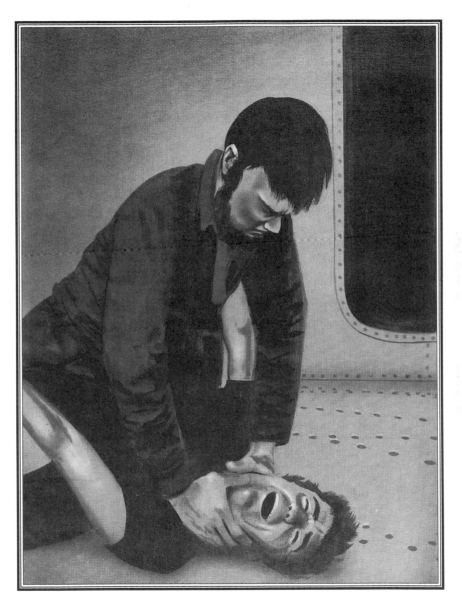

"Tell me the truth, Professor. Wouldn't your captain just as soon have chased and shot at a submarine as a sea monster?"

I had no answer. Commander Farragut would have thought it was his duty to destroy such a submarine, if he had known it existed.

"I have the right," he went on, "to treat you as prisoners of war. You may roam as much as you want around this ship, but you can never leave it!"

With these words, the commander led me from the cell into a big room. I gasped with surprise. It was like a museum!

"I see that you like my collections, Professor," he said, smiling. "Let me welcome you aboard the submarine *Nautilus*. You may call me Captain Nemo."

I thought that the name suited this strange man, because *nemo* was the Latin word for "no one". He continued to speak.

"For many years I have collected the marvels and riches of the sea. Here you will find samples of many things that museums back on land would pay fortunes for. I think that as a scientist you may enjoy your stay with me, sir."

I looked around and knew that he was right. As a scientist interested in the sea, a trip in the *Nautilus* would be a golden chance for me. There were beautiful sea shells in glass cases. There were stuffed fish and other sea animals. The walls were covered with fine paintings. And at one end of the room, there was a large organ.

But best of all there were two big windows. I could see hundreds of fish swimming past the *Nautilus!*

Next to this room was a library with thousands of books. I could see that Captain Nemo was a scientist too.

"Tell me, Professor," he said. "Was your study at the Paris museum this quiet and peaceful?"

"I have a thousand questions, Captain!"

"Please have a seat, and I will try to answer them."

"First, I would like to know where you came from, and why you built this wonderful submarine."

"Who I am is of no concern to you. You only need to know that I am someone who has decided to be done with the human race, for reasons which I will not tell. I no longer have any contact with land. I get everything I need from the sea."

"You must love the sea," I said.

"Yes, I love it!" he replied, "The sea is everything! The air is pure and healthy, and a man need never be lonely here. Life is stirring all around him. The sea belongs to no one. Men can fight their wars on its waves, but thirty feet down, all is peace. Only here can I find freedom. Only here do I have no masters. Here I am free!"

"That is why you built the *Nautilus*?"

"Yes, I built it on a desert island. I found men who thought as I do. They became my crew."

"What powers the *Nautilus*? I have seen no sign of a steam engine."

"For the answer to that you must come with me again."

Captain Nemo led me down a long hall into another room. It was the engine room of the submarine. Huge machines were humming.

"Everything on the *Nautilus* is run by electricity,

Professor."

"Electricity!" I cried.

"Yes, from very powerful batteries that I made myself. Electricity runs these motors. It gives us light and we even cook with it."

"How do you gather your samples for your museum? How do you get your food?"

"I was just about to invite you and your friends to join me on a trip."

"A trip?"

"Yes, at the bottom of the sea!"

Captain Nemo led me to a small room, where I met Conseil and Ned. Here Nemo and one of his men showed us how to get into some heavy rubber diving suits. Nemo showed us some round metal tanks.

"These contain air. You wear them on your backs, and these hoses carry the air into your helmets. There is enough air in the tanks for several hours."

"Will we have any weapons?" asked Ned.

"Yes," replied the Captain, "These guns fire special bullets. The bullets are like little batteries. They will shock anything they touch."

The helmets were put on our heads. The door to the room was sealed and the room began to fill with water. As soon as it was full, another door was opened. We stepped out onto the floor of the ocean.

It was a wonderful experience to walk underwater. The plants and coral looked like a garden of flowers. The hundreds of fish that swam around my head looked like butterflies. They were every color of the rainbow. Behind me was the big, black shape of the *Nautilus*, with its bright

lights gleaming.

It was an amazing experience for me. All my life I had studied the creatures that live in the sea, but never before had I been able to see them alive in their own world. Truly, Captain Nemo's ship was wonderful!

We walked for many miles, until even the bright lights of the submarine were gone. Everywhere I looked, I saw something marvelous. However, one time I was reminded that dangerous things live in the sea too. As I walked around a big piece of coral, I was suddenly facing a giant sea spider! It must have been three feet high. It had very large claws. It was ready to spring at me!

Captain Nemo hurried past me and knocked the monster over with the butt of his gun. I hurried away as fast as I could.

Soon we returned to the *Nautilus*. I heard the motors start and the submarine began to move.

I spent the next few days reading some of the many good books in the Captain's library. I also studied the fish that swam past the windows. Conseil helped me take notes. Ned, however, was not very happy. He was an outdoor type, a harpooner, and he did not like being shut up inside.

One day, as I was peacefully reading, there was a crash, and the whole submarine shook. Had we run into something?

Captain Nemo came into the room.

"An accident, Captain?" I asked.

"In a way, Professor," he answered. "We were going through some reefs and have run aground on one. We will have to wait for the tide to float us off."

I went up onto the deck of the submarine. The jagged rocks of the reef were all around us. Nearby was a small island. The Captain had followed me onto the deck. I asked him, "Do you think that we might be able to go ashore for a few hours? We cannot escape from that small island. It would do Ned good to visit dry land for a while."

"Of course," he said. "I'll get the boat ready for you."

Ned was very happy to learn that he could go hunting on the island, even if it was only for a few hours. He was getting very tired of eating fish all the time. The little rowboat took us to the island quickly.

We hiked far into the jungle. We were able to find some birds that we shot for our dinner. We also found some fruits and vegetables to take back to the *Nautilus*. We were talking about what a wonderful meal we were going to have back on board, when suddenly a stone fell at our feet!

"What was that?" cried Ned.

Just then, a second stone knocked a bird from Conseil's hands.

"Savages!" he cried.

Sure enough, twenty natives ran out of the wood waving spears and knives. They did not look friendly.

"Run!" shouted Ned.

Our boat was about sixty feet away. We ran for it as fast as we could. Stones and arrows fell all around us. We threw everything we had into the boat and jumped in. We pulled away from the beach just as the natives ran into the water. They couldn't swim after us.

"That was a close call!" said Ned.

"We'd better tell Captain Nemo," replied Conseil.

When we got back to the submarine, I went below to find the Captain. He was busy taking notes.

"Well, Professor, did you have a good hunt?" he asked.

"Yes, but we brought some bipeds back with us."

"What bipeds?"

"Savages!"

"There are savages everywhere, Professor! How many were there?"

"At least a hundred."

"There could be a thousand. The *Nautilus* would have nothing to fear!"

I went back onto the deck, where Ned and Conseil still were. The natives had left the beach. Now there was something worse. They had gone to get their own boats. A dozen big canoes were crossing the water toward us. Each canoe was filled with shouting natives, shaking their spears at us! Soon spears and arrows began to land on the deck, so we ran below. I went to the Captain again.

"You had better close the hatch, Captain!" I said.

"Why?" he asked.

"Because there are a hundred natives out there who would love to come down inside and kill us!"

"There is nothing to worry about," said Captain Nemo.

"But the hatch is open!"

"They won't come in," he said. I couldn't see why not, so I went to the hatch to see what would happen. The first native who tried to set a foot on the ladder suddenly gave a loud yell and jumped straight up into the air! The same thing happened to the next native, and the next one!

"What's happening?" asked Ned, and he went to climb the ladder. As soon as he touched it, he cried out in pain and was thrown onto his back.

"The ladder is electrified," said Captain Nemo, coming up behind us. "It will give a powerful shock to anyone who touches it. That is why the natives are afraid to come aboard!"

"Well, it certainly works!" said Ned, rubbing his arm.

The Captain turned off the electricity and we went up onto the deck. The natives had all gotten back into their canoes and had gone away. Before long, the tide came in and the *Nautilus* floated off the reef. We were on our way again.

We cruised for many days without anything exciting happening. Sometimes we sailed on the surface, and sometimes we went underwater. Even though I knew that I was a prisoner, I was happy. I was seeing so many wonderful things. I didn't really care if I ever got back home. As for Conseil, he was a loyal assistant. As long as he was with me, he was happy too. It was Ned who worried me. The longer he kept inside the submarine, the unhappier and angrier he got. Escape was all that he could think of. I was sure that sometime he would do something that would get us all in trouble.

As we were crossing the Indian Ocean, I saw an amazing sight through the windows. The sea all around us was glowing. There were millions and millions of tiny jellyfish in the water, and when they were disturbed by our passage, they glowed brightly, like fireflies. They were a living light!

Not long after that, Captain Nemo came to my room.

He looked very upset.

"Professor," he asked me, "You are a doctor too, aren't you?"

"Yes, I am," I said. "Is something wrong?"

"I'm afraid so. Can you come with me?"

"Of course," I said, and followed the Captain. He took me to a part of the submarine I hadn't seen before. It was the crew's quarters. A man was lying on one of the bunks. There was a very bad injury to his head. I looked at him, then took Captain Nemo to one side, where the injured man couldn't hear me.

"Will he live?" asked the Captain.

"No, I am afraid not. He will be dead in just a few hours."

I saw tears form in the eyes of a man I had thought didn't care about people. "Thank you, Professor," he said. "You may return to your room."

A few hours later, the Captain came to my room again. He asked if Ned, Conseil and myself would please join him in another underwater trip. We agreed. Soon we were walking across the ocean bottom again. We came to a large open area, and I was suddenly aware that there were crosses made from coral everywhere. It was an underwater cemetery! I then saw that some of the men with us had been carrying a large object. I now knew that it was a coffin. It was put down into a hole, which was then filled in with more coral. The Captain and his men bowed their heads for a few moments. Then we returned to the ship.

A few days after that sad scene at the underwater cemetery, Captain Nemo once again invited us on a trip. We were near Ceylon, where there are large pearl

fisheries. The Captain thought that it might be interesting to see how pearls were gathered. We put on our suits again, and left the submarine. As the water was very shallow, we could see the surface only a few yards over our heads.

When we reached the pearl fishery, we watched how the divers worked. They would tie heavy stones to their feet, jump into the water, and gather as many oysters as they could. when a diver ran out of breath, he untied the stones and swam back to the surface.

We were about to leave when a dark shadow passed over our heads. It was a huge shark! It was headed straight for one of the divers. As it circled the poor man, it struck him with its tail. The diver was knocked out and sank to the bottom. The shark turned to attack. Just then, Captain Nemo leaped in front of the shark. He had his knife in his hand and grabbed onto one of the shark's fins.

It was the most thrilling battle I had ever seen! I can still see the brave Captain Nemo, standing there. He braced himself and waited for the shark to attack him. When it rushed at him, he quickly threw himself to one side. Then he stabbed the shark with a dagger. Blood poured out of the side of the shark. It was so thick, I could hardly see the captain. When I saw him, he was holding on to one of the shark's fins.

A terrible fight followed. The shark seemed to rear with its huge open mouth. Its teeth were terrible to see. The shark moved so fast, it made the water hard to stand in. I wanted to help the captain, but I was too afraid to move. The shark opened its mouth to bite the captain. They rolled over and over. Just when I thought the Cap-

tain was lost, I saw his knife again plunge into the side of the shark. Clouds of blood poured forth. The giant shark sank to the bottom. Captain Nemo brought the diver to the surface and put him back into his boat. He checked to be sure that the man was still alive. The diver would be amazed when he woke up and found himself back in his boat!

On the way back to the submarine, Captain Nemo took me aside. We walked a few yards, into a little grotto. There, on a big lump of coral, was growing the largest oyster I had ever seen. It must have been over six feet wide. The Captain pried open the shell. I gasped at what I saw inside. It was a pearl the size of a baseball! I must have been worth millions of dollars. The Captain carefully closed the shell and we joined the others.

I had one more mystery about Captain Nemo to solve. Why did he care so much about his crewmen and the pearl diver, yet he would ram and sink war ships?

We continued our trip. We entered the Red Sea. While cruising on the surface, Ned suddenly became very excited, and pointed out to sea.

"What is it, Ned?" I asked.

"It's a dugong!" he cried.

As we got closer I saw that he was right. A dugong is a huge animal, something like a walrus. They are sometimes called "sea cows". Ned begged the Captain to let him chase the creature. The Captain gave him permission to use the small boat. He allowed some of the crew to row for him. Soon, harpoon in hand, Ned was in full pursuit. It wasn't like hunting whales, which is what Ned was most used to, but it was the next best thing. It was an exciting

chase.

The dugong which Ned was hunting was huge! He took careful aim and threw his harpoon with all of his might.

"I have missed it!" cried Ned.

"No," I said. "The dugong is wounded. You can see its blood in the water." The dugong came to the surface again. Its wound did not make it weaker. Again Ned threw his harpoon at the animal. This time he did not hit it. We chased the dugong for an hour. It was a very fast swimmer, and almost got away. It dove under the water, and we couldn't see it.

Suddenly, it turned and charged at the boat. "Look out!" cried Ned. The dugong threw itself at the boat, nearly tipping it over. We were almost tipped over, but Nemo's men righted the boat. The dugong charged again. Ned was very angry with the animal. He finally got close enough to strike. He returned to the submarine a happy man. At least for a little while.

The *Nautilus* passed through a secret underwater tunnel that connected the Red Sea with the Mediterranean. Soon we were near the island of Crete. It belonged to Greece, said the Captain. Greece had been captured by its enemy, Turkey. Many Greeks were trying to revolt against the Turks and get their country back. But the Greeks were very poor, and couldn't buy weapons or help. As the Captain was telling us this, Conseil suddenly cried out in surprise. We went to the window to see what it was. There was someone swimming outside! When Captain Nemo saw him, he gave a signal which the swimmer answered.

Then the swimmer rose to the surface of the water.

"Do not be alarmed," said Captain Nemo. "This man is a bold diver. He is more at home in the water than on the land."

"Do you know this man, Captain?" I asked.

"I do," said Captain Nemo. He turned and rang a bell. Several strong crewmen came in and carried out a large iron chest which I had seen sitting on the floor.

"What was that?" I asked.

"Gold," replied the Captain, "to help the Greeks."

"Gold!" I said, "There must have been hundreds of pounds in that chest! Where could you get so much gold?"

"If you really want to know, I will show you!"

I had to wait several days, until we left the Mediterranean and were sailing up the coast of Spain. The *Nautilus* stopped and Captain Nemo asked me to get into my diving suit once again. The Captain, several of his men, and I, left the submarine. We walked a mile or two, then I saw them — sunken ships, many of them. They looked very old, as though they had been there for hundreds of years. Then I saw what Captain Nemo's men were doing. They were carrying chests from the ship. I knew then what these ships were. They were Spanish treasure ships! Each one carried millions of dollars of gold, silver and jewels. We were visiting Captain Nemo's private bank!

When we got back to the ship, Captain Nemo looked at me. "Did you know that the sea had such riches?" he asked.

"I knew that there were many shipwrecks in this sea," I said.

"There are wrecks here, and in many other seas," said the captain. "But to get the treasure from them would cost

most men more than the treasure is worth. I only have to bring my ship here and pick up the treasure. I am a very rich man, Professor Aronnax."

"It is a shame that the treasures will only be kept here. If men were to find them, they could do good with such wealth," I said.

The captain grew very angry. "Do you think that I pick up this money for my own good?" he cried. "Do you think that I don't care for the pain of other people? Who told you that I do not make good use of it? Do you not understand?" He stopped. He seemed to wish that he had not spoken so much.

I understood. The money which Captain Nemo's men picked up from the wrecks was put to use to help people. He gave it to people like the Greeks, who were fighting to keep the Turks out of their country. What made the captain leave the land I did not know. I could see that he still cared for people.

A few days later I was invited on another underwater trip. What amazing thing was the Captain going to show me now? He and I went alone this time. It was a very long walk over rough ground. I was getting tired. However, I was very curious about a strange glow I could see ahead. It got brighter as we got closer. As we came around a bend, I could finally see what caused the light. It was the eruption of an underwater volcano! And at the base of the mountain, lit by its flickering glow, was a city! It was in ruins, destroyed when it sank beneath the sea thousands of years ago.

I could see fallen buildings, There were ruined statues lying down and temples. It was amazing! But what city

could this be, lost beneath the waves all these centuries? Captain Nemo could see that I was confused. He took a piece of chalk and on some black rock wrote one word: ATLANTIS.

It was the legendary city that the world thought was only a myth, a fable. Yet here it was before me!

Ah! Why did I have such little time? I would have liked to walk through this lost city. What history was lying here! I would have liked to have seen the buildings of its people. I would have liked to study their great city and seen how they lived. But I knew that I must go back to the ship soon. The walk had been long. I would run out of air soon. All the way back to the submarine I thought about what I had just seen. The ruined buildings, with open roofs and fallen temples, broken arches and pillars lying on the ground were quite a sight! I also thought about what Captain Nemo had been thinking. Would he have liked that ancient world better than this modern one?

Back in the *Nautilus*, the Captain told me that the batteries of the ship were getting low, and that he had to stop at his base to recharge them.

So Captain Nemo had a base! This would be interesting news for Ned! Where could the base be? Some secret island perhaps? We would soon find out.

After a day or so had gone by, Captain Nemo told me that we had come to his base. I went up onto the deck. But what was this? It was the middle of the day, yet it was almost all dark! I looked straight up. There was a bright blue circle over my head, like a huge moon. I knew then what it was — a circle of daylight. We were in some kind of cave. There was a round hole in the roof that was letting light in.

Captain Nemo made it clear to me. His secret base was inside an extinct volcano. An underwater tunnel let into it. The volcano was hollow. The circle of daylight I could see at the top was the volcano's crater.

Captain Nemo let Ned, Conseil and me go ashore while his men worked on the batteries. This almost drove Ned mad. There could be no escape from this island, since the walls of the cavern curved overhead. There was no way to climb them.

We hunted the seabirds that nested on the rocks and gathered some eggs. Soon we returned to the submarine. Ned was angry at the trick the Captain had played on him.

The next day the *Nautilus* was in a strange part of the Atlantic Ocean. It was an area called the Sargasso Sea, a kind of sea-within-a-sea in the middle of the Atlantic. It was large, and shaped like a circle, where seaweed grew very thickly. Legends told of ships that had been trapped there, unable to escape. However, in real life, the weed did not grow thickly enough to be any real danger.

We wandered around the Atlantic for several days. Nothing really thrilling happened. Then Captain Nemo came to my cabin and asked,

"Would you care to see how deep the *Nautilus* can go?"

"Yes, I would!" I said.

The Captain gave some orders. A few minutes later I could feel the submarine sinking.

"We are at a spot," said the Captain, "where scientists could not find the bottom even with a line 42,000 feet long."

"How deep are we now?" I asked.

Nemo's secret island *draw*
somewhere in the South Atlantic
...al to extract sodium from...

2000

GRAND OCÉAN

PACIFIQUE

13 March, 1868   Pierre Aronnax

The Captain looked at an instrument on the wall. "We are almost that deep now!"

I looked out the window. It was very dark. All I could see were a few black peaks rising from below. The *Nautilus* still sank, and I could hear its iron plates groaning under the huge pressure of the water.

"We are at a depth now of about 48,000 feet. That's about nine miles deep."

"Look at those strange rocks out there!" I said, "There is not a single living thing at this depth!"

"Would you like to take a picture to remember this by?" the Captain asked.

"Can we do that?"

"Yes indeed" he said, going to a cabinet on the wall. He brought back a large camera and tripod. He set it up so that we could take a picture through the window. I still have the picture we took.

"We had better go up to the surface now," said Captain Nemo. "I don't want to keep the *Nautilus* under so much pressure from the water for too long."

He gave a signal. "Hold on!" he said. I barely had time to do so when the *Nautilus* shot up like a balloon. We were going through the water so fast, the submarine was shaking! In just four minutes we went up the eight or nine miles to the surface! The *Nautilus* shot out of the water like a flying fish. Then it fell back onto the waves with a huge splash.

A few days later Ned, Conseil and I were sitting on the deck. Ned was telling us how bored he was. I could understand how he felt. He was a man of action, not a book lover like Conseil or myself. Think of his great joy when he sud-

denly spotted a school of whales! He ran to the Captain, to ask if he could hunt them. But he was very upset and angry when the Captain said no.

"There goes a whole fortune for a whaling ship!" Ned cried.

"I am not a whaling ship" the Captain said to him.

"You allowed me to hunt the dugong," Ned said.

"That was different. We needed the meat. We have no use for the meat of these whales."

"Can't I chase them, just to remind myself what it's like to be harpooner?"

"What for?" asked the Captain. "Just to kill them? That would be killing just for the sake of killing. I don't approve of killing for sport. Already whalers are killing off whole species of animals. Soon there will be none left!"

There was nothing that Ned could say to make the Captain agree. He had to watch the herd of whales swim peacefully away. From that day on I noticed that Ned's hatred of the Captain grew greater. I promised myself to watch him closely.

Day after day the *Nautilus* went further and further south. Was Captain Nemo going to take us to the South Pole? I couldn't believe that even he would go that far. But soon, we soon saw icebergs floating near us. The blocks of ice kept getting bigger and bigger as we kept going south. Soon the *Nautilus* was slipping through huge sheets of ice that covered the water. It was getting very cold outside. Fortunately the inside of the submarine was kept warm.

The ice became so thick that I was afraid the *Nautilus* would become trapped. I told the Captain of my worry.

"Don't worry, Professor," he said. "The *Nautilus* will

go farther south yet!"

"Farther south!" I cried. "Are you going to take us to the South Pole?"

"Of course!"

I thought that the Captain was mad. But hadn't he already showed us that the *Nautilus* could do amazing things? Why couldn't it take us to the Pole?

"But," I asked him, "how can even the *Nautilus* get over hundreds of miles of ice?"

"Not over Professor, but *under*".

Now I understood what he was going to do! Beneath the ice was open water, we would sail beneath the ice cap to reach the South Pole. It was a wonderful idea.

"But what if there is thick ice at the Pole? How can we go to the top of the water for air?"

"That is a chance we'll have to take!"

The *Nautilus* dived. Very slowly it slipped beneath the ice. We had to go very carefully. If we crashed into the bottom of an iceberg, we could wreck the submarine.

Every once in a while there would be a bump when we would strike the bottom of the ice. We kept having to go deeper and deeper, as the ice above us got thicker and thicker. There was no sign of the ice thinning as we neared the Pole. Already the air inside the submarine was getting bad. What if we couldn't get to the top of the water at the South Pole? How could we get any fresh air? If it took too long to reach the Pole, we would run out of air!

Captain Nemo tried several times to rise to the surface, but each time he bumped against the ice. Finally, he broke through. We all rushed onto the deck. The *Nautilus* floated in the middle of a huge sheet of ice, as far as the

eye could see. The Captain looked at the stars, and measured the position of the *Nautilus*.

"Are we at the Pole?" I asked.

"Not yet," he said.

Again the *Nautilus* went under the water. The next time it came to the surface, there was open water around it, like a big lake surrounded by icebergs. Not far from us was a group of rocks. Captain Nemo took the small boat and rowed to the rocks. He climbed onto them and took another measurement.

"Is this the Pole?" I asked.

"I will know in a moment," he said, as he studied the stars.

Soon Captain Nemo looked up and said in a serious voice, "The South Pole!"

At these words he took out a large black flag. As it waved in the cold wind, I saw that it had his initial, "N", on it in gold. I asked him, "In whose name are you claiming the South Pole?"

"In my own!" he said. Then he returned to the boat, as the last rays of the setting sun sparkled on the waves. A night six months long spread its shadows over Captain Nemo's new land.

The ship got ready to leave. As the long night began, it became very cold. The stars twinkled brightly in the freezing air. New ice was beginning to form around the *Nautilus*. We had to leave very soon, or we would be frozen in!

The submarine soon sank beneath the waves and we were under way. In a day or two we would be free of the ice. It would be none to soon, as far as I was concerned!

I was quietly sleeping in my room the next morning when I was awakened by a loud crash. I was thrown from my bed onto the floor. I ran from my room, looking for the Captain. I found him in his museum.

"What happened?" I asked.

"An accident, I'm afraid," he said.

"A serious one?"

"Perhaps," he said, looking a little worried. "As we were passing beneath an iceberg it turned over, trapping us under it."

"Can we get out?" I asked.

"We shall see!"

He went to his instruments and ordered the *Nautilus* to move ahead slowly. After a few moments there was another crash. The *Nautilus* had run into something blocking it from the front. Captain Nemo then called for his submarine to go in reverse. Once again we only moved a short distance before we ran into something.

"What does this mean?" I wanted to know.

"It means that we cannot escape by going up or down, forwards or backwards!"

"We are trapped then?"

"Yes!"

I went to tell Conseil and Ned the bad news. They wanted to know what was going to happen.

"I don't think that we will starve," I said. "There is plenty of food. I am worried about the air. We only have enough for forty-eight hours. If we cannot escape in two days, we shall die!"

"What does the Captain plan to do?" Ned asked.

"I don't know," I said.

"Well, let's ask him!"

We returned to the museum where the Captain was busy with ideas. We told him what we wanted to know.

"There is one chance," he said, "The iceberg is too thick above us and to the front and sides, but it may be very thin beneath us. If we can make it a little thinner, the *Nautilus* may be able to break through."

"How can we do that?" we asked.

"We will have to go outside in our diving suits and dig a hole beneath the submarine! All of us will have to take turns working."

It was very hard work, trying to dig through the ice with picks and shovels. The water around us was freezing, making our work even harder. Even with all of his crew working, and with our help, at the end of the first day the hole was not deep enough.

We worked all through the night, taking turns going out. The air inside the *Nautilus* was getting very hard to breathe. We only had one day left! We were all getting so tired, we could hardly move. But we had to keep working!

Our 48 hours were almost up. I was in the museum, gasping for breath. Our air was nearly gone. Captain Nemo came in.

"Is the hole deep enough?" I asked.

"I don't know," he said. "We will have to try to break through anyway. It's our last chance!"

He ordered that the ballast tanks be filled with water. He hoped that they would make the *Nautilus* heavy enough to break through the ice.

There was a loud cracking sound! The *Nautilus* suddenly lurched. I could feel it sinking! We had broken

through! Captain Nemo gave the order to surface. Quickly, the submarine shot upward. As soon as it was on the surface, the hatch was thrown open and everyone rushed onto the deck. The fresh air felt wonderful! It was great to breathe again!

I didn't ever want to get that close to dying again. But just a few days later, when we were back in the Atlantic Ocean, we had another adventure!

Conseil was looking out the window when he asked, "Professor, how big do squids get?"

"I have a friend," I replied, "who once saw one that was more than fifteen feet long."

"Well, if this is not the one your friend saw, then it must be its brother!"

I rushed to the window. I saw a horrible sight! Not only was there one giant squid, there were seven! Suddenly, the *Nautilus* stopped moving. Captain Nemo came in and I asked him what had happened.

"One of the squids has gotten caught in the propeller. We have to go to the surface and get rid of them."

"Can we shoot them?"

"No, the electric bullets won't work on them."

We were soon on the surface. As soon as the hatch was opened, a long tentacle came slithering down the steps like a snake. Captain Nemo chopped it off with a hatchet and went up the ladder. We followed him.

It was a frightening sight on the deck! There seemed to be hundreds of long, curling arms everywhere! Some of us struck at them with our hatchets, while others, like Ned, used harpoons.

Suddenly, I saw a squid's arm wrap around Captain

Nemo. He was lifted off his feet! In a moment he would be lost. He would be carried under the water by the monster! Quickly, Ned threw his harpoon at the squid. It was a perfect hit! The creature dropped the Captain as it slid from the deck.

Soon, all the monsters were either dead or dying. The deck of the *Nautilus* was slippery with their strange, green blood.

Before we went back down the ladder, Captain Nemo took Ned by the hand.

"You saved my life," he said to the harpooner, "Why?"

"I don't know!" replied Ned.

From that day, Captain Nemo seemed very different. He kept away from us. He stayed by himself and didn't speak. Something was worrying him.

When we reached the North Atlantic, we were suddenly hit by a powerful storm. Instead of diving underwater, where it was safe, Captain Nemo stayed on the surface. He even rode out the storm on the deck. Giant waves crashed over him. Lightning flashed all around. I thought that he was trying to kill himself!

One day, Ned, Conseil and I found out what had been worrying the Captain. There was a ship following us!

"The *Abraham Lincoln* must have gotten back safely," I said. "It must have told the people that it was not a monster that was attacking ships, but a submarine! Now everyone is looking for the *Nautilus!*"

I must have been right, for every day the ship got closer. Ned was very curious about what nation the ship belonged to. He got a telescope from the museum, and

took it onto the deck. But no sooner had he raised it to his eyes, than the Captain struck it from his hands. I had never seen Captain Nemo so angry!

"Get below!" he cried.

"Are you going to attack that ship?" I asked.

"I'm going to sink it!" he said

"But whose ship is it?"

"You don't know? Good! Now get below!"

A few of his crew came at his order and made us go down the ladder. We gathered in the museum. Soon we could hear the shots form the ship's cannons.

"They're shooting at us!" said Conseil.

"What is the Captain going to do?" asked Ned.

"He's going to ram that ship!" I said. As I spoke I could feel the *Nautilus* suddenly pick up speed. We were going faster and faster. Captain Nemo aimed his submarine at the attacking ship like a missile.

It hit the ship with a loud crash! The *Nautilus* was going so fast, it passed through he warship like a needle going through cloth!

The ship sank with everyone on board.

From that day on we did not see Captain Nemo. He kept to his room. The *Nautilus* seemed to wander without any captain. Where were we? We couldn't tell. Ned thought that this was the time that we should try to escape.

Finally, we chose one dark night. We would steal the little boat that was on the deck of the *Nautilus*. Since the Captain never came out of his room, he wouldn't notice until it was too late. We would be gone.

It was dark inside the submarine as we crept from our

rooms. Suddenly I heard a sound. It was music. Captain Nemo was in the museum playing his organ! Would he notice us?

We knew that we had to go through the salon in order to escape. My heart beat fast. I opened the door of the salon very quietly. It was dark in the salon. I crept silently behind the captain. I do not think he would have noticed us if the lights had been on in the ship. He was very involved in the music he was playing. If he were to see us, all would be up!

Slowly and quietly we sneaked to the ladder that led to the deck. Just then, I heard the last words I ever heard Captain Nemo speak.

"Almighty God!" he said, "Enough! Enough!"

We opened the hatch and went onto the deck. It looked as though there was a storm outside. Giant waves swirled around us. The *Nautilus* rolled like a bucking horse, and we could hardly hold on.

"It's a whirlpool!" cried Ned, "Get in the boat before it sucks us all down!"

Just as we got in, the *Nautilus* began whirling around faster and faster. Suddenly it threw the boat off the deck like a stone from a slingshot. I hit my head, and that's the last thing I remember.

I awoke in a fisherman's hut. Ned and Conseil were there. What had become of Captain Nemo and his *Nautilus*? Did they disappear in the whirlpool? Did they escape? No one knows, but I hope so!

About Captain Nemo

When Verne styled his first draft of Captain Nemo, the captain was a Polish patriot who hated the Russians because they had killed his family in the rebellion of 1863. Jules Hetzel, the publisher, vetoed this idea since the political climate between France and Russia was touchy and there was no reason to antagonize the Russians.

Thus, Nemo appears without a firm nationality. His handwriting is "Germanic", his dark complexion suggests to Aronnax a Mediterranean birthplace, he supports the Greek rebels and claims a brotherhood with the Indian pearl fisherman. His monogram "N" recalls that of the French emperor, Napoleon Bonaparte. Finally, in *The Mysterious Island*, Verne reveals Nemo's birthplace — but that is a secret for you to read there.

Was Nemo modeled after a real person? Robert Fulton, the inventor of the original *Nautilus* in 1800, has been suggested as have Colonel Charras, who opposed Napoleon III, and Albert I of Monaco, a great oceanographer. The Russians have linked Nemo with Gustave Flourens, supporter of the Greek revolt. Even Sherlock Holmes nemesis, Professor Moriarty, has been mentioned. Perhaps, Nemo is a composite of all these people, plus Verne himself, who shared the Captain's great passion for "music, freedom and the sea."

ABOUT THE ILLUSTRATOR

Ron Miller was born in Minneapolis, Minnesota in 1947. He is one of the best known science-fiction artists in America. His paintings are on display by NASA (National Aeronautics and Space Administration), the Smithsonian Institute, and even the Pushkin Museum in Russia! Many of his paintings have been seen in magazines and on book covers. He has also written some books on science-fiction art.

Twenty Thousand Leagues Under the Seas is Ron's first book for the Unicorn Publishing House. He began to love the story after watching the Walt Disney movie. At home, he has a large collection of Jules Verne's works – nearly 300 books! Ron lives in Virginia with his wife and six cats. He is looking forward to illustrating many more books for The Unicorn Publishing House.

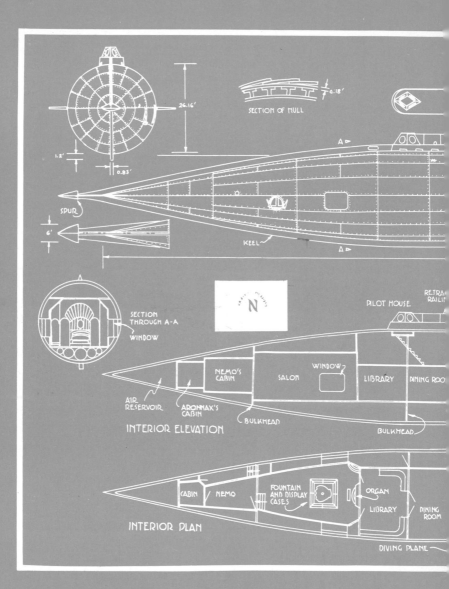